RIDE, FLY GUY, RIDE!

Tedd Arnold

SCHOLASTIC INC.
New York   Toronto   London   Auckland
Sydney   Mexico City   New Delhi   Hong Kong

Ride, Wally, ride!

Copyright © 2012 by Tedd Arnold.

Library of Congress Cataloging-in-Publication Data

Arnold, Tedd.
Ride, Fly Guy, ride! / Tedd Arnold. -- 1st ed.
p. cm.
Summary: While riding in the car with Buzz and his father,
Fly Guy gets blown out of the window and finds himself riding in a truck,
then a boat, a train, an airplane, and maybe even a rocket.
ISBN 978-0-545-22276-1
[1. Flies--Fiction. 2. Transportation--Fiction.] I. Title.
PZ7.A7379Rid 2012
[E]--dc23

2011020179

ISBN 978-0-545-22276-1

10 9 8 7 6   15 16 17/0

Printed in Malaysia   108
First edition, January 2012

A boy had a pet fly.
He named him Fly Guy.
And Fly Guy could
say the boy's name—

Chapter 1

One day, Dad said, "Who wants to go for a ride?"

"We do!" said Buzz and
Fly Guy.

"Everyone buckle up!"
Dad said.

Then they hit the road with the windows down.

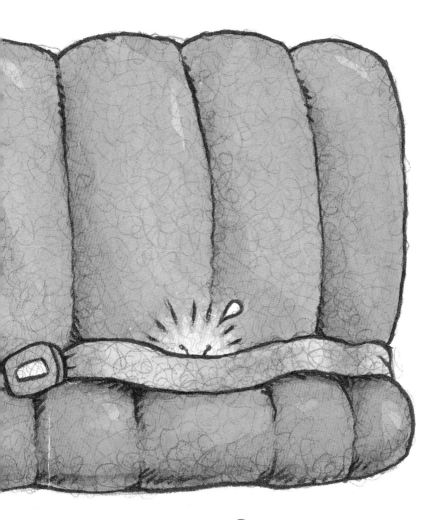

Buzz stuck his hand out the window and pretended it was an airplane.

Suddenly, wind blew in the car and carried Fly Guy out of the window . . .

. . . and into a passing truck.

Chapter 2

"Follow that truck!"
cried Buzz.

Meanwhile, in the truck,
Fly Guy tumbled into
the truck driver's mouth.

The truck driver spit Fly Guy

out the window . . .

. . . and into a passing
motorboat.

"Follow that boat!" cried Buzz.

Meanwhile, on the boat, Fly
Guy saw a man put a bug on
a big hook.

Fly Guy jumped overboard . . .

. . . and onto a passing circus train.

"Follow that train!" cried Buzz.

Meanwhile, on the train,
Fly Guy surprised a sleepy
elephant.

The elephant blew him off
the train . . .

. . . and onto an airplane.

"Follow that airplane!"
cried Buzz.

Meanwhile, on the airplane, the pilot saw Fly Guy and turned on the wipers.

"Follow that . . . I mean, follow Fly Guy!" cried Buzz.

Just then,
a rocket
roared up
from the
ground.

Chapter 3

"Follow that rocket!" cried Buzz.

Buzz and Dad landed. The rocket raced into space. "Will Fly Guy survive?" asked Buzz.

"Fly Guy, you're here!" cried
Buzz. "The rocket didn't
take you to space!"

Dad said, "Let's ride home."
And Fly Guy said—

MORE RIDEZZZ!